Police
Cat Fuzz

Karen Wallace

Illustrated by
Trevor Dunton

For Paul and Nancy

PUFFIN BOOKS

Published by the Penguin Group
Penguin Books Ltd, 27 Wrights Lane, London W8 5TZ, England
Penguin Putnam Inc., 375 Hudson Street, New York, New York 10014, USA
Penguin Books Australia Ltd, Ringwood, Victoria, Australia
Penguin Books Canada Ltd, 10 Alcorn Avenue, Toronto, Ontario, Canada M4V 3B2
Penguin Books (NZ) Ltd, Private Bag 102902, NSMC, Auckland, New Zealand

On the World Wide Web at: www.penguin.com

Penguin Books Ltd, Registered Offices: Harmondsworth, Middlesex, England

First published 2000
3 5 7 9 10 8 6 4

Text copyright © Karen Wallace, 2000
Illustrations copyright © Trevor Dunton, 2000
All rights reserved

The moral right of the author and illustrator has been asserted

Set in Plantin

Printed in Hong Kong by Midas Printing Limited

British Library Cataloguing in Publication Data
A CIP catalogue record for this book is available from the British Library

ISBN 0-141-30201-1

Fuzz wanted to join the police force because he was tough, smart and it was time cats had a chance to catch criminals.

If dogs could do it, why not cats?

So Fuzz put up a poster in the roughest part of town.

WANTED!
PARTNER FOR POLICE CAT
MUST BE TOUGH AND SMART
AND MUST LIKE CATS!

Then he hid in a dustbin and waited.

I

A few minutes later, Sergeant Malcolm walked by.

He had huge feet and carried three truncheons.

It is a well-known fact that the best policemen have huge feet so that they can stamp out trouble, fast.

Also, you can't juggle with less than three truncheons and Sergeant Malcolm was an ace juggler.

Sergeant Malcolm read the poster.

Fuzz watched as twirling truncheons rose and fell in the air.

Sergeant Malcolm caught his truncheons, one, two, three.

"Sounds good to me," he said. "If dogs can do it, why not cats?"

3

It was exactly what Fuzz wanted to hear.

He jumped out of the dustbin and rubbed his head against Malcolm's knee.

They looked each other in the eye and understood each other completely.

Then they cycled down to the police station on Sergeant Malcolm's bicycle.

"This is most unusual," said Inspector Long Arm. "But if dogs can do it, why not cats?"

It was exactly what everybody wanted to hear!

Inspector Long Arm leaned forward. "Get me the Rat and the Wrestler behind bars by sundown and you have got a job."

Sergeant Malcolm didn't move.
Police Cat Fuzz didn't blink.

The Rat and the Wrestler were the sneakiest crooks around. And no one could catch them because the Rat and the Wrestler were masters of disguise.

Police Cat Fuzz purred hard in Sergeant Malcolm's ear.

"We'll get them, sir," said Sergeant Malcolm.

Some people say policemen understand their dogs so well, it's as if they can speak to each other.

With Sergeant Malcolm and Police Cat Fuzz, there was no "if" about it.

"Colliding cat nuts!" said Police Cat Fuzz, as he climbed on to the back of Sergeant Malcolm's bike. "Where shall we start?"

"Tubby Stick's chocolate factory," replied Sergeant Malcolm. "Somebody's stealing the chocolate and I think I know who it is!"

Suddenly, an old lady pushing an enormous pram stepped into the road in front of them.

Sergeant Malcolm swerved and
slammed into a post box.

Police Cat Fuzz landed upside down
in a tree.

"Watch where you are going,"
bellowed the old lady.

"Some of us are trying to sleep!" a
voice screeched from inside the pram.
Then they zoomed off and shot round
a corner.

"Old people, today," hissed Police Cat Fuzz. "Some of them have no manners at all."

Sergeant Malcolm stared at his bicycle. The wheel was bent and the light on the front was broken.

"There was something funny about that baby," said Police Cat Fuzz. "It had a pointed furry nose. It looked just like a rat."

"There was something funny about that old lady," said Sergeant Malcolm. "She had hairy arms. She looked just like a wrestler."

"Look!" cried Police Cat Fuzz.

A silver bar was lying on the pavement.

"It must have fallen out of their pram."

Police Cat Fuzz stared at the silver bar. TUBBY STICK'S CHOCOLATE was stamped on the side. He pulled out his magnifying glass and saw two sets of prints. One was of a huge hand with fat fingers. The other was of a paw with tiny claws. It was the Rat and the Wrestler, no doubt about it.

"Now all we have to do is catch them," muttered Sergeant Malcolm.

A pink Rolls-Royce pulled up beside them and a movie star climbed out. She had golden hair, hairy arms and long white gloves.

"Poochy! Poochy!" she squawked. "Have you seen my little Poochy?"

Sergeant Malcolm removed his

helmet. "Who is your little *Poochy*?" he asked politely.

"My darlingest pet," sobbed the movie star. She pointed with her fat white finger. "Look! Look! He was over there!"

Sergeant Malcolm looked.

Police Cat Fuzz looked.

Suddenly the car door slammed shut and the Rolls-Royce roared off.

"Movie stars," muttered Sergeant Malcolm. "No manners at all."

Then he remembered her hairy arms and fat white fingers. She looked more like a wrestler than a movie star.

Police Cat Fuzz was thinking about the driver. He had two furry ears poking out of his cap.

He looked more like a rat than a
driver.

Police Cat Fuzz stared down at the
pavement.

The silver bar of chocolate was
gone!

Sergeant Malcolm stood outside Tubby Stick's chocolate factory tossing his truncheons in the air.

Sergeant Malcolm had his best thoughts when he juggled.

"I know!" he cried. "We'll use Tubby Stick's factory as a trap for the Rat and the Wrestler!"

Police Cat Fuzz felt his fur stand on end. *"Purrfect,"* he whispered.

Ten minutes later, Tubby Stick listened in horror at their plan.

"Open Day at my chocolate factory?" he wailed. "What if the Rat and the Wrestler steal all my chocolate?"

"They won't," said Sergeant Malcolm grimly.

"We'll be waiting for them," growled Police Cat Fuzz.

"All right," groaned Tubby Stick. "I'll do it!"

An hour later, a huge sign hung from the factory windows.

CHOCOLATE FACTORY
– OPEN DAY –
EVERYONE WELCOME

"Ready?" said Sergeant Malcolm.

"Ready," replied Police Cat Fuzz.

Sergeant Malcolm stood behind a pillar.

Police Cat Fuzz hid in a tree.

Hundreds of people began to arrive. Some were fat and some were thin. Some were bearded and others were bald-headed. Some wore fancy clothes and others wore plain ones.

But there was only one stagecoach. A cowboy with a pointed nose sat on top. A princess with hairy arms sat inside! The cowboy jumped down.

"That's them!" hissed Police Cat Fuzz.

They peered inside.

The Rat and the Wrestler were looking at a plan of Tubby Stick's factory!

CHOC FACTORY
PLANS

"We'll take them by surprise,"
whispered Sergeant Malcolm.

They jumped into the stagecoach
and slammed the door behind them.

Quick as a flash, the Rat and the
Wrestler jumped out the other side.

There was a horrible *click* as hidden
locks slipped into place.

Police Cat Fuzz and Sergeant
Malcolm were trapped!

"Don't worry!" cried Police Cat
Fuzz. "My lock pick is in my collar!"

Police Cat Fuzz pushed the pick into the lock.

He twisted it.

He turned it.

He wiggled it upside down.

Nothing worked.

"Let me try," said Sergeant Malcolm.

WHACK!

With his huge feet, Sergeant Malcolm kicked down the door.

"Follow me!" cried Police Cat Fuzz. He raced over to a manhole.

Sergeant Malcolm lifted the cover and they climbed down inside.

Within seconds they were crawling along a tunnel underneath the factory.

"How will we catch them?" puffed Sergeant Malcolm.

"Leave it to me," said Police Cat Fuzz with a low growl.

They came to a huge room with metal gates. "That's the chocolate safe," whispered Police Cat Fuzz.

He twisted the pick in the lock.

The gates swung open.

Sergeant Malcolm and Police Cat Fuzz tiptoed into the safe. On both sides, stacks of silver chocolate bars towered up to the ceiling.

At that moment, the Rat and the
Wrestler appeared around the corner.
They were driving forklift trucks!

"Hurry!" hissed Police Cat Fuzz.
"You hide behind one stack. I'll hide
behind the other."

Sergeant Malcolm grinned. "And
when they're in the middle —"

"We'll push!" said Police Cat Fuzz.
Which is exactly what they did!

Inspector Long Arm couldn't believe his eyes.

"The Rat and the Wrestler are behind bars," said Sergeant Malcolm.

"Underneath them, actually," said Police Cat Fuzz.

"Congratulations!" cried Inspector Long Arm. "You both deserve a medal."

"How about these?" asked Tubby Stick. He held out a tray of brand new chocolates. There were two kinds. A crunchy *Police Cat Fuzz* and a creamy *Sergeant Malcolm*!

Police Cat Fuzz purred with pride.

Sergeant Malcolm went pink with delight.

Everyone said they were the best chocolates ever!

Except the Rat and the Wrestler!

They said they didn't like chocolate any more!